Spellmakers

Julie Rainsbury

Illustrated by
Graham Howells

PONT BOOKS

First Impression—1999

ISBN 1 85902 631 1

© text: Julie Rainsbury
© illustrations: Graham Howells

This book is published with the support of the
Arts Council of Wales.

Printed in Wales by
Gomer Press, Llandysul, Ceredigion

CONTENTS

The Book of Spells

A famous wizard called Dafydd Llwyd once lived near Ysbyty Ystwyth. His magic powers were known far and wide throughout the countryside. People often asked him to cast spells bringing health, bountiful harvests, wealth and happiness to themselves, or to cast curses bringing sickness, failed crops, poverty and misery to their enemies. Dafydd Llwyd didn't care which sort of magic he was asked to make. Good or bad, the people paid him just the same.

Dafydd Llwyd had a servant boy called Siôn. Siôn cleaned the wizard's house, but he was never allowed to dust the bottles, phials and caskets which contained ingredients for magic. Siôn cooked the wizard's meals, but he was never allowed to stir the cauldron which bubbled day and night with secret potions over the fire. Siôn tidied the wizard's papers, but he was never allowed to open the great Book of Spells, which was bound with iron bands and chained to a high shelf in the wizard's library.

Dafydd Llwyd had a horse called Taran. The horse was huge. When he galloped, his mane and tail streamed out like clouds at evening, his eyes were pools of darkness, his flanks midnight. Some people claimed he could soar into the sky. They said his hooves struck lightning through the trees. They said his silhouette crossed the moon's full face with Dafydd Llwyd mounted on his back.

Every morning, Dafydd Llwyd went into his library. He climbed the special library ladder and unlocked the chain and iron bands from the Book of Spells with an ornate key. He carried the great book to his desk. It was covered in crimson leather and had a five-pointed star embossed in gold on the front. Dafydd Llwyd was always careful to shut the library door before he opened the Book of Spells.

Siôn was forbidden to enter the room while the wizard was working but often, when he passed in the corridor, he could not help hearing voices. The voices puzzled Siôn because he knew that the wizard always entered the library alone.

'Who can he have in there with him?' Siôn wondered, day after day.

He dared not ask the wizard. Dafydd Llwyd would not be pleased to be questioned and Siôn had been told that it is never wise to upset a wizard.

Every afternoon, having studied his spells and eaten his dinner, Dafydd Llwyd would call for his horse. Taran shone like jet in the sunlight and sparks flashed as he pawed the cobbled yard. Siôn's legs were prickled by fire as he held his master's stirrup. Dafydd Llwyd heaved himself high into the saddle and Siôn was allowed to lift the precious Book of Spells towards him. The wizard would lean down to take the heavy book and wrap his cloak carefully around it before galloping off on his spell-casting, curse-casting, visits.

One afternoon, Dafydd Llwyd was asked to call on an important family who lived high in the hills above the River Ystwyth. The daughter of the house was very ill and the family hoped that the wizard's spells would be able to cure her. Siôn helped Dafydd Llwyd to mount Taran as usual.

When the wizard had gone, it was quiet in the yard. Siôn pulled some carrots from the kitchen garden. He carried them into the house, enjoying the fresh smell of the earth that clung to them. He tumbled them into the stone sink, ready to scrub for the wizard's supper. It was then that he noticed it. The Book of Spells glowed, red and gold, like some weighty jewel, against the dark wood of the table. Forgotten.

Siôn wondered what to do. Dafydd Llwyd would be furious when he realised that the Book of Spells had been left behind. He was quite likely, in a temper, to blame Siôn for the mistake and Siôn had been told that it is never wise to upset a wizard.

Siôn tucked the Book under his arm and set off after Dafydd Llwyd. The day was hot. The mountain road was rocky and dusty. The Book was very heavy. After a while, Siôn had to stop to rest. The mountains were bare, apart from the occasional wind-bent tree. The shallow-rooted grass was bleached almost white by the sun. Below him the River Ystwyth sparkled as it gushed and swirled past boulders in the valley.

The sight and sound of the water made Siôn feel even more hot and thirsty. The Book lay uncomfortably across his knees. The leather was warm to his touch but, when he ran his fingers down the edges of the thick, roughly-cut pages, they seemed strangely cold. Their coolness was tempting, as if to open them would be a relief. The sun beat down on Siôn's head, making him sticky and slightly dizzy. He brushed a fly away from his forehead. He felt very strange. He flicked the pages of the Book of Spells. They fluttered through his fingers like snowflakes. He watched the pattern of their shade across his hands.

Slowly, as if in a daze, Siôn opened the Book wide.

A shape rose up in front of him, like a shadow, like smoke. It seeped out from the open pages of the Book of Spells. Siôn shrank back. The shape became more solid – a dark, crooked creature with bat's wings, buzzard's beak, owl's eyes, toad's skin. The creature jabbered at Siôn. It was the voice that Siôn had heard in Dafydd Llwyd's library.

'What shall I do, master? What shall I do?'

Siôn knew that spirits who live in magic books, like genies who live in magic lamps, have to be given tasks to do at once. Siôn glanced anxiously around him. There was not much to occupy a magic spirit on the bare mountain. The creature jabbered more loudly.

'What shall I do, master? What shall I do?'

Siôn looked down into the valley. The creature's voice was now a screech that set Siôn's teeth on edge.

'What shall I do, master? What shall I do?'

'Lift the boulders out of the river,' said Siôn in desperation.

The creature flew down the valley. Soon boulders were being tossed onto the riverbank as if they were pebbles. The crashing and rumbling of rocks made a noise like thunder. The din was deafening. At last there were no boulders left in the water and the River Ystwyth flowed broad and smooth.

'What shall I do, master? What shall I do?'

Siôn realised that, now he had released him, he had no idea how to get the creature safely back into the Book of Spells.

'What shall I do, master? What shall I do?'
Siôn was in despair.

'What shall I do, master? What shall I do?'
The voice went on and on – a sharp shriek like chalk against slate.

'Throw the boulders back into the river,' said Siôn, hoping to give himself time to think.

The creature flew down the valley. Soon boulders were being tossed back into the river as if they were pebbles. Water splashed in high, gleaming arcs. Rocks crunched and scraped against each other. The din was deafening.

Suddenly the valley darkened. Siôn looked round. Taran stood on the ridge behind him and Dafydd Llwyd was mounted on his back, blocking out the sun. The wizard had heard the wild tumult that sounded like a battlefield and had ridden back to investigate. He saw at once what had happened. He saw at once that Siôn was to blame. The shape of the wizard grew vast and menacing against the skyline, dark as storm cloud. The wizard urged Taran into a gallop. They thundered down the mountainside towards the guilty boy.

Siôn cowered beside a stunted tree. There was nowhere to hide from Dafydd Llwyd's fury. The wizard shouted an incantation and the spirit was immediately lifted into the air, dropped onto an open page and the Book of Spells was slammed shut.

Taran and Dafydd Llwyd skidded to a halt in front of Siôn. The wizard's face was twisted with anger. He raised his arm to curse Siôn. Taran reared, thrashing his hooves. Lightning ripped through the branches of

the stunted tree and a shower of twigs and leaves and rowan berries descended on Siôn. He clutched frantically at a bunch of berries. He hardly knew what he was doing but somewhere he had heard that the rowan tree was a protection against witches and wizards. The berries were scarlet in his hand – a red brighter and more vivid than even the crimson of the Book of Spells.

Dafydd Llwyd rode round and round Siôn. He scowled, he shouted, he cast his worst spells but he could not harm the servant boy who held the spray of rowan fast in his fist. At last, the wizard gave up and road away, taking his Book of Spells with him.

Siôn never went back to work for Dafydd Llwyd, but always, all his life, he made sure that he carried a sprig of rowan with him. Siôn had learnt his lesson. Always, all his life, he told everyone he met – he told his wife, he told his children, he told his grandchildren – that it is never, ever wise to upset a wizard.

The Witch and the White Cow

A long time ago, on the border between England and Wales near Corndon Hill, there was a terrible drought. Day after day, the sky was blue and cloudless. Day after day, the sun glittered cruelly and air shuddered with heat above the dusty roads. Day after day, week after week, month after month, there was no rain. Rivers dried to a trickle and crops shrivelled in the fields. Farm animals grew thin and died, until the people thought they would soon die too, unless help came.

The only person who did not seem at all worried by the famine was a woman called Mitchell. The garden around her cottage was green and lush. Vegetables grew in plump rows, trees were heavy with fruit and flowers bloomed by her front path. But she did not share any of her good fortune with her needy neighbours. She smirked a secretive smile to herself and sang a song softly under her breath. The song's words were a murmur that no one could quite catch. She flitted about her garden in a long, red cloak – vivid as poisonous berries in a hedgerow.

The people muttered against her. Every morning they would look at the sky and then towards Mitchell's cottage.

'No clouds,' said one. 'We're bewitched.'

'No rain,' said another. 'We're bewitched.'

'No hope,' said a third. 'We're bewitched.'

Day after day, the people's despair grew greater and their hunger harder to bear.

One morning, just when they thought they could go on no longer, the people saw a white shape growing against the sky on the top of the hill behind Mitchell's cottage.

'It's a cloud,' cried one. 'Magic!'

'Rain's coming,' cried another. 'Magic!'

'It's a cow,' cried a third, 'and it must be magic. Only a fairy cow could be so white, so dainty, so shining.'

The white cow could be seen clearly now. The sun glittered fiercely but it only made the cow more dazzling and cast a cow-shaped shadow down over Mitchell's garden.

The people gathered their pots and pans, their bottles and bowls, their jars and jugs and started to climb the hill. The cow stood still on the summit as the long line of people flowed slowly up the track towards it. Their voices babbled excitedly and their containers clinked like pebbles on a riverbed jostled by water.

The cow stood still on the summit and one after another the people crouched down to milk her. All day she stood and each bucket and mug, pail and ladle, kettle and dish that was brought to her was filled to the

brim with creamy milk. The people carried their containers carefully home and turned their faces away from Mitchell's cottage when they passed.

Mitchell sat in her garden and scowled as she watched them. Her garden was chill in the cow's shadow. Her song was a sliver of ice in her throat and her teeth chattered with cold, with anger. She drew her cloak about her and shivered. Its bright scarlet was dulled to the colour of rust or bloodstain.

Day after day, Mitchell brooded in her garden as the people climbed the hill. Day after day, she brooded as they returned with their bowls of brimming milk. Still no rain came but the people were no longer hungry. They laughed now as they passed Mitchell's cottage.

'See how her flowers droop in the shade,' said one. 'The spell must be breaking.'

'See how her face is frozen in a frown,' said another. 'The spell must be breaking.'

'See how our fairy cow blazes on the hill like a beacon,' said a third. 'The spell must be breaking.'

Mitchell brooded. She brooded through dawn, day and dusk. She brooded through the night while the cow stood drenched in moonlight on the hill, her horns sparked with stars.

The next morning Mitchell joined the queue to climb the hill. She climbed slowly and people moved aside to let her pass. No one wanted to be too close to her. Mitchell wore her long, red cloak which glowed dangerously, like fire, in the sunlight. She climbed awkwardly, with her head and back bent, as if she carried something hidden beneath her cloak.

At last Mitchell stood beside the fairy cow. The cow was cold light, polished as silver. Mitchell was burnished, her cloak billowing flames of colour around her. Mitchell reached among its folds and drew out an enormous, metal colander.

The people nearest to her roared with laughter.

'Stupid Mitchell,' said one.

'You can't collect milk in a colander,' said another.

'It will all run out of the holes,' said a third.

Mitchell smirked her secret smile and crouched down to milk the fairy cow. She murmured her strange song, softly, as if to herself. Mitchell milked steadily. As fast as she milked, so the milk poured out through the holes of the colander and was wasted on the ground.

The people began to mutter to each other.

'Move over,' said one.

'You'll never be done,' said another.

'Let someone else have a turn,' said a third.

Mitchell smirked her secret smile and went on milking. She milked through dawn, day and dusk. She milked all night. The people were angry and hungry and afraid.

Mitchell went on milking. She chuckled to herself, sure that she had outwitted the cow's magic and that the people would now starve.

Mitchell went on milking. She milked for days, for weeks, for months and the milk poured through the colander.

It was lonely on the hill. The people no longer came to ask her to stop and the cow just stood still and white and silent on the summit.

'Surely they're all dead by now,' Mitchell thought at last. 'They've had nothing to eat for ages.'

She stopped milking and flexed her fingers. She stretched her aching back and knees and turned to look down into the valley.

Mitchell let out a scream of fury.

The valley spread out below her was green and fertile. The milk pouring through the colander had run down the hillside filling the dry riverbeds. The land had blossomed. The fields were full of crops, animals could be seen grazing and the people were happily busy about their work. The valley was back to normal and the people had almost forgotten about Mitchell sitting milking the fairy cow on top of the hill.

Mitchell screamed again – a long, lingering, high-pitched wail. People in the valley lifted their heads, puzzled. Mitchell raised her arm and struck out at the cow beside her. There was a crack like thunder, a blinding flash like lightning.

People in the valley pointed and started to run towards the hill. When they reached the summit, the fairy cow was nowhere to be seen. But where Mitchell had been, a group of standing stones had appeared which had never been there before. The people studied them, wondering. The stone in the centre of the group was shaped like a woman, her back rather bent, her arm raised as if to strike, an expression of fury mixed with terror on her face. The other stones were arranged around her like a pen or sheep-fold, like a prison to keep her in.

Many years have passed since a fairy cow has appeared on the borders of England and Wales, but near Corndon Hill a group of standing stones can still be seen and local people call them 'Mitchell's Fold.' The stone in the centre is very ancient and weathered but some say they can still see the shape of a woman in it. The spot is lonely and, day after day, the wind shrieks strangely across the hillside like a scream.

Aby Biddle and the Bees

Almost two hundred years ago, in the south of Pembrokeshire, a vicar and his wife were preparing for a party. The vicar's wife flapped all day like a hen in a panic.

'What a mess! What a mess!' she clucked to the servant girl who was sweeping the stairs, washing the windows, capturing the cobwebs and buffing the brass. She knocked over the girl's bucket as she scurried by, sending a splash of grimy water across the floor.

'What a mess! What a mess!' she clucked to the cook who was baking the bread, peeling the potatoes, filleting the fish and juggling with jellies. She knocked over the cook's bowl as she scurried by, sending a stream of beaten egg across the floor.

'What a mess! What a mess!' she clucked to the parlour-maid who was cleaning the cutlery, placing the plates, gathering the glasses and fiddling with flowers.

She knocked over a vase as she scurried by, sending a shower of bruised petals across the floor.

The vicar had shut himself away in his study.

'Peace, perfect peace,' he purred to himself as he thought about writing his sermon.

Just before the guests were due to arrive, he came out to inspect the arrangements.

'Alleluia!'

He beamed at the rooms bright as heaven.

'Alleluia!'

He beamed at the food fit for a feast day.

'Alleluia!'

He beamed at the table fine as any altar.

The vicar's wife preened, as if she had done it all herself.

The vicarage was set in a lonely spot and the winter night was cold. The servants lit candles and stoked up the fires. A flurry of snowflakes fell as the first guests began to arrive.

Everyone who was anyone had been invited, from the squire to the schoolmaster. Among the guests was Aby Biddle, the most famous wizard in Wales. It was not often that he was tempted out from the secluded valley where he lived. Many of the people at the party had heard of his reputation as a sorcerer, a magician and a conjurer, but had never met him before.

The vicarage was soon full of gaiety and laughter. The guests ate the fine food and drank the fine wine and the logs blazed cheerfully in the fireplace. Outside, snow continued to fall. A blanket of crisp quietness covered the drive, the lawns, the beehives on the edge of the vegetable garden, the woods and fields beyond. As the night drew on, the talk turned to fairy tales, ghost stories and magic.

'No such thing as magic,' said the squire.

He thumped his plump hand on the arm of his chair and his white neckerchief gleamed in the candlelight.

Aby Biddle sat by the window and twisted the fringe of the curtain between his fingers. He smiled to himself.

'Superstitious nonsense,' said the schoolmaster.

Aby Biddle drew back the edge of the curtain and looked out over the garden. His smile grew broader.

'Quite right! Alleluia!' said the vicar.

Aby Biddle noticed that it had stopped snowing. The moon cast a circle of light, like a golden disc, on the silver-surfaced snow of the lawn. Aby Biddle turned his wide smile on the company.

'Watch me,' he said.

Aby Biddle pushed open the casement window and stepped outside. He glided across the lawn, leaving no footprints in the snow. He scooped up the circle of moonlight and glided towards the beehives. He bent to the side of each hive, his ears full of the hum and slumber of bees. He held the disc of light above him like a halo. He called to the bees.

'Dewch, dewch, dewch.'

The guests listened fearfully from the open window. They knew, as everyone knows, that bees understand Welsh.

'Dewch, dewch, dewch.'

Aby Biddle continued to call softly as he glided toward the house. A skein of bees followed him. A skein that grew thicker and longer by the minute.

Aby Biddle stepped back into the room. He placed the ring of moonlight, bright, in the middle of the floor.

'Dewch, dewch, dewch.'

He chanted the words again, loudly now, and bees streamed through the window into the circle of light. As each one landed, it grew huge and glistening. More and more bees filled the room. Each bee grew enormous. The room thrummed with their sound. Bees swarmed over the plump hands and white neckerchief of the squire. Bees tangled, angry and shrill, in the beard of the schoolmaster. The floor, the walls, the table, the ceiling were thick with bees.

'What a mess! What a mess!' squawked the vicar's wife. 'A....A....A....'

The vicar didn't know what to say. Alleluia, for once, did not seem quite the right word.

Aby Biddle grinned at the vicar.

'Abracadabra?' he suggested.

The room was in uproar, filled with screaming guests and buzzing bees. The turmoil seemed to go on for ever.

At last, Aby Biddle bent and cast the disc of moonlight out through the window. The bees flew after it. The bees grew smaller and their hum more distant. Then all was quiet again.

'Ladies and gentlemen,' said Aby Biddle.

His smile stretched from ear to ear as he bowed to each corner of the room. 'Perhaps you all now believe in magic.'

He caught up his cloak, brushed a few stray bees from its lining, and stepped out again into the night. His demonstration of wizardry was over and his boots crunched into the snow, making deep footprints as he set off down the drive.

The other guests hurriedly took their leave. There was a great hullabaloo as they shouted for their horses and carriages. Eventually everyone had gone and only a single bee buzzed on the hearth. The vicar's wife shuddered as her husband brushed it into the fire. She surveyed the ruined room – the tipped chairs, the fallen wine-glasses, the remains of food on the table.

'What a mess! What a mess!' she clucked as she went to call the servants. She knocked over a dish as she scurried by, sending a trickle of trifle across the floor.

The vicar crossed the room and closed the window, shutting out night and bees and sorcery. He shook his head, which still buzzed like a hive, and slumped into a chair. At last the noise inside his head was silenced. He sighed shakily, gratefully.

'Peace, perfect peace,' he purred.

The Lady of the Wood

A man called Einion went to live near Tregaron with his wife, Angharad. He built a mansion on the banks of the River Teifi which he called Ystrad Caron. He was a kind and generous man and he also built a bridge over the river, at his own expense, to help his poorer neighbours. Einion was contented in his new home. He farmed his land and often said he loved nothing on earth as much as his wife and his harp. Einion was one of the best harp-players in Wales and he owned the most magnificent harp. The instrument was so fine that only he could draw a sound from it. In the evenings, Einion would play for his wife as they sat together by the fire.

One day, Einion was walking through a wood which grew near his mansion when he heard a wonderful sound. The wood was full of birds but this new, fluid call entranced him.

'Surely,' thought Einion, 'it must be the song of the nightingale.'

Einion had read many poems about nightingales, but he had never heard one singing in the local wood before.

That night he was distracted as he played his harp. Its music no longer satisfied him. He seemed to hear the distant echo of the nightingale's song behind every note.

'What's the matter?' Angharad asked.

'Nothing,' said Einion.

He didn't know how to explain the sudden discontent he felt. The nightingale's song trilled in his head, elusive and bewitching. Einion left the harp and sat next to his wife. He took her hand in his and patted it. Their matching rings, bands of pale gold, glinted in the firelight.

Each day, Einion went to the wood. He couldn't stay away. Each day, he heard the nightingale's call. He followed the sound deeper and deeper into the wood. Each day, the wood seemed to grow denser and wilder. It seemed to go on forever.

In the evenings, Einion tried to play his harp as usual but the music sounded dull to him now. His head was full of birdsong. He always stopped playing after just a short time.

'What's the matter?' Angharad asked each evening.

'Nothing,' said Einion.

Einion had no time for anything now except roaming the woods. He explored further and further. The nightingale's call led him on. One day, he pushed through some branches into a clearing. He could see no sign of the bird he sought, but its song was louder than ever in his ears. Suddenly, the strangest and loveliest woman he had ever seen appeared through the trees.

Her skin was pale as may blossom, her lips red as rowan berries, her eyes the violet of alder buds. Her hair was burnished, copper-gold, like beech leaves in autumn. She was slender as ash, graceful as the boughs of wych elm, scented with lime and elder flower. Her clothes were glossy with leaf-greens: blue green, yellow green, grey green. Her cloak unfurled around her, trailing a rainbow of woodland flowers. Their names whispered through the clearing like a spell:

tormentil, foxglove, pimpernel,
herb-robert, primrose, hellebore,
yellow archangel, wild strawberry,
speedwell, enchanter's nightshade,
celandine, campion, bluebell,
sweet woodruff, lily of the valley.

When the lady spoke, her voice was the song of the nightingale. When she told it, her name was full of the echoes of oak—*deri*, *derw*, *derwen*. On her head she wore a rare crown of mistletoe and the ground around her feet was starred with ramsons.

As she moved towards him, Einion glimpsed the shadow of a hoof beneath the hem of her skirt but he was lulled by the music of her voice. She took his hand and he walked with her as if in a dream, bedazzled.

Einion lingered with the lady of the wood. He watched leaves unfold on the trees, watched thin catkins shake their pollen into the wind. Blossom foamed around him. He moved like a sleepwalker under a canopy of green. The woods went on forever. Sometimes he walked through scratches of bilberry, bracken and heather. Sometimes he waded by streams where kingfishers flashed, sudden and vivid as memory, on the far edge of his sight. Einion watched ferns turn to rust, followed the spiral of wind-whirled seeds, saw leaves blaze like fire and fall.

The lady was always with him. Sometimes she was spun in butterflies, pearl and silver fritillaries. Sometimes bees hummed through her honey hair. At dusk, moths, brindled and mottled umber, fluttered around the flame of her presence.

Each night, Einion rested on cushions of moss. He watched the moon wax and wane above birch, rowan and ash, above alder, willow and hawthorn, above oak, holly and hazel, above tangles of bramble and ivy, above the dry rattle of reeds and the crooked shape of the dark-berried elder.

One night, Einion lay awake and watched the bare branches of the trees move against the sky. The moon was full, a pale-gold circle. A breeze sighed through the reeds of a small lake. The sound was sad, full of loss and some long-forgotten music. Einion looked at the lady. She stood at the water's edge, evergreen, berry-lipped. Her beauty glittered fiercely, sharpened by frost. The mistletoe shone in a bright circlet on her head. Einion caught his breath as he saw her dip a dark hoof in the water and slowly stir the ring of the moon's reflection.

Einion twisted the gold band on his finger. Suddenly it seemed precious. It spun in his mind like something he was about to remember. All at once he knew that he had to protect the ring.

Einion slid the ring from his finger. He opened his right eye wide and slipped the ring under his eyelid to keep it safe.

Einion blinked and looked around. The scene was different. It was as if looking through the ring made him see things clearly for the first time. The trees were tight around him, dark and menacing. Their trunks enclosed him like the bars of a prison. The water of the lake looked cold and leaden now and waves sucked greedily among tree roots at its margin. At first Einion thought the lady had gone. Then he heard the pounding of hooves and a monstrous shape lunged towards him. It was snouted and bristled as a boar, hooved and antlered as a stag, yellow-eyed and yellow-fanged as a wolf. The seductive song of the nightingale was lost in the raucous screech of a bird of prey.

Einion turned to flee. His heart was beating as loud as the thudding hooves behind him. Einion dodged and ducked through the wood. Branches of birch beat at him as he ran, wands of ash pierced and tore his clothes, tentacles of willow clutched at his ankles. Giant hawthorns reared in his path, armed with dangerous spikes. Reeds arrowed at his legs. Einion slewed through blackberry bushes, scratching his face and arms. He was elbowed and battered by trunks and twigs and branches. Einion raced on. The sound of hooves was never far behind. Sometimes the creature was so close that he felt its hot breath on his neck.

At last Einion reached the edge of the wood. He tore out of the shadow of the trees. He ran across his river bridge and didn't pause for breath until he reached the

wall that enclosed the mansion garden. Then he turned
and looked back.

The vast wood was shrivelling before his eyes. The trees
disappeared from the landscape like a puddle drying in
the sun. Soon, just the bare bones of the hills were left.

Einion looked down at his torn clothes and scratched
skin. He could see the end of a straggling beard and the
hair of the beard was grey. He began to wonder how
long he had been under the spell of the lady of the wood.
He remembered seasons passing, but in the wood he
had always been young. Now Einion realised that his
back was bent and his knees ached with age.

He let himself quietly into the mansion through the
kitchen door. The cook was busy kneading dough and
didn't notice him pass through. Einion made his way up

to the living room. An elderly lady sat beside the fire. A dusty harp stood in the shadow of the chimney breast. Einion moved slowly to the harp. He flexed his cramped fingers. He struck a ripple of notes from the strings. Angharad looked up. She knew her husband at once, despite the years that had passed since he had disappeared, despite his grey beard and ragged clothes. No one, she told him, had been able to pluck a note on the harp since he left.

Einion sat next to his wife and patted her hand and their matching rings, bands of pale gold, glinted in the firelight. He smiled to himself.

'What's the matter?' Angharad asked.

'Nothing,' said Einion. 'I was just thinking that I love nothing on earth as much as my wife and my harp.'

In the years that followed, Einion continued to farm his land and to be admired by his neighbours. He still went for his daily walk but he was glad that the wood had disappeared. He grew to enjoy the open uplands, the freedom of the wide views that remained. Scatterings of the great wood still lingered here and there in spinneys and dingles, in hedgerows and at the edges of churchyards, but Einion was careful to avoid them. As for the song of the nightingale, its enchanting call has never been heard again in those parts, from that day to this.

Merlin's First Magic

After he had been defeated in battle, King Vortigern retreated to the mountains of Snowdonia and ordered his men to build a tower to protect his new camp. He found a perfect site. It was like the roof of the world – rocks tickled the clouds and only eagles could soar higher.

At dawn, teams of builders set to work. They dug trenches, mixed mortar and shaped great blocks of stone which they heaved into position. By evening, the foundations of the outer wall were finished. The builders rubbed their aching backs and packed away their tools. They sniffed the promise of supper cooking in pots over the camp fires.

Suddenly, the ground shuddered under their feet. There was a roar – like thunder, like fire, like anger – that seemed to come from the very centre of the mountain. The men trembled. They clung to each other, tumbled, clutched at tussocks of grass on the quaking ground. The mountain growled, was shrill with clanging like the clash of battle armour. Earth churned and boulders rumbled away to shatter in the valley. The builders watched in horror as the stone foundations of the tower began to crack and crumble. Soon, all the day's work lay in ruins around them. Then the din stopped as unexpectedly as it had begun. There was a final skittering of pebbles and then the mountain stilled.

Day after day, the same thing happened. Each morning the builders would start work but each evening, whatever they had built would be destroyed. Everyone became very frightened. King Vortigern called his magicians to him and demanded to know the cause of the problem.

'The mountain is angry, lord,' said the first magician, 'and you must bring it a gift. Only a snow-white unicorn with a horn of ivory and a golden mane will do.'

The king sighed. The first magician always said that a unicorn was necessary when he didn't know what to do. The king had heard tell of unicorns, but no one had ever found one. He called his second magician.

'The mountain is angry, lord,' said the second magician, 'and you must bring it a gift. Only a mermaid with hair like sunshine on water and a tail the deep, blue-green of oceans will do.'

The king sighed. The second magician always said a mermaid was necessary when he didn't know what to do. The king had heard tell of mermaids, but no one had ever found one. He called his third magician.

'The mountain is angry, lord,' said the third magician,
'and you must bring it a gift. Only a giant with a beard
like brambles and a voice louder than thunder will do.'

The king sighed. The third magician always said a
giant was necessary when he didn't know what to do.
The king had heard tell of giants, but no one had ever
found one.

And so it went on. The king summoned magician after magician and each of them said a gift was needed to please the mountain, but each gift was more fantastic and impossible to find than the one before.

In despair, the king called his thirteenth and last magician to him.

'The mountain is angry, lord,' said the thirteenth magician, 'and you must bring it a gift. Only....'

The magician paused and thought frantically. His fellow magicians had already used up most of the usual list of impossible gifts.

'.... only .... a young boy who has no earthly father will do,' he ended triumphantly.

The thirteenth magician felt rather startled. That was not what he had meant to say at all. It was as if some other voice had spoken through him.

'Hrmph.'

The king stared hard at the thirteenth magician.

'Still .... a boy, you say? At least that might be easier to find than some of the other ideas. He'd have to be killed to please the mountain, I expect?'

'Oh, most certainly, most certainly, lord,' said the thirteenth magician. 'There would have to be blood to please the mountain.'

The king sighed. His magicians always suggested that something or somebody had to be killed when they didn't know what to do.

'Oh well,' said the king. 'I suppose we can try.'

The king's messengers travelled the length and breadth of the land. At each town, village or farmstead they announced their quest.

'In the name of Vortigern, we seek a boy who has no earthly father.'

And at each town, village and farmstead, the people laughed at them. Even if there were boys whose fathers had died or boys whose fathers had disappeared, those boys were always sure that their fathers had been human.

At last, worn out, dusty and discouraged, the king's messengers arrived at the gates of Carmarthen town. As they dismounted, a scuffle broke out among some boys who had been playing with a ball in a meadow beside the River Towy. Their quarrelling voices carried clearly to the king's men on the still, evening air. A dark, slim youth scooped up the ball and began to walk away towards the town.

'As for you,' one of the other lads called after him, 'we don't want to play with you anyway. No one even knows who you are, for you never had a human father.'

The king's messengers looked at each other, their tiredness forgotten. They tethered their horses and followed the boy into the narrow streets. After twisting through lanes and climbing steep alleys, the boy ducked through a doorway close to St.Peter's church. The king's men followed him.

A woman sat by a fireside in a low room. The king's men declaimed their usual message.

'In the name of Vortigern, we seek a boy who has no earthly father.'

The woman started.

'Oh Merlin, my son, I knew a call would come for you one day.'

41

Merlin looked coldly at the king's messengers.

'I have no earthly father. What do you want of me?'

The messengers explained about Vortigern's tower and what the king's thirteenth magician had suggested.

'The blood of a boy,' scoffed Merlin. 'What nonsense. I can show the king's magicians that a boy is more powerful and knowing than they are. My father was indeed magical. He could be any creature of air, land or water: eagle, stallion or sewin. He was dream and myth beyond your imagining, his name too powerful to be spoken. Other magicians bowed down like grass at his passing. I am his son.'

After several days of hard travelling, the king's messengers brought Merlin to Vortigern. The king stood in front of his ruined tower and his magicians were gathered around him. Merlin turned furiously to the magicians.

'Why do you suggest remedies to your king which you know are useless? Why do you want my blood when you have no idea why his work is destroyed? It is not the mountain that is angry but the dragons that live and fight beneath it.'

The magicians muttered amongst themselves.

The king sighed. Obviously Merlin was going to be one of those magicians who always talked about dragons. The king had heard tell of dragons. The king had heard tell of dragons more often than he cared to remember. Dragons were always being blamed for things but the king had yet to meet anyone who had ever seen a dragon.

Merlin spread his arms.

'Beneath this mountain there is a lake,' he said.

His voice was low and calm. His body seemed to flicker. One moment he was tall as a man, like his father before him, like himself to come. The next moment he was Merlin the boy.

The king's builders dug into the ground below the ruins of the tower. They dug for a week and, at the end of that time, a great lake appeared, cupped in the bowl of the mountain top.

Merlin spread his arms.

'Beneath this lake there is a stone chest,' he said.

The king's builders started to drain the lake. They drained for a week and, at the end of that time, a stone chest appeared resting in the empty bowl of the mountain top.

Merlin spread his arms.

'Beneath this lid there are dragons,' he said.

The king's builders chiselled away at the clasps that bound the stone chest. They chiselled for a week and, at the end of that time, the stone lid sprang open and revealed two dragons coiled asleep. One dragon was white with scales that held the sheen of moonshine. One dragon was red with scales that held the flare of sunrise. As they watched, the dragons woke up and began to fight. They roared as they scratched and tore at each other. Their fiery breath scorched the bowl of the mountain. The stone chest clattered and scraped against the rocks. Their scales clashed as they lashed their tails at each other. The noise was hideous. The whole mountain was shaken by the power of the battle.

At length, the dragons' fury ended and they coiled once more into the stone chest.

Graham Howells

'The white dragon represents the Saxons,' Merlin told the king, 'and the red dragon, the Britons. Their battle is like the continual war between the two peoples. You will get no peace here and your tower will never stand.'

Merlin spread his arms.

The lid of the stone chest closed of its own accord. Slowly it disappeared as the bowl of the mountain brimmed once more with water. Rocks and earth tumbled back into place until even the lake was hidden, as if it had never been.

King Vortigern decided to take Merlin's advice and choose a different spot to make his stronghold. Just to be on the safe side, he moved his army, his builders and his thirteen foolish magicians much further south. He built his castle quite close to Carmarthen, in a place still known today as Craig Gwrtheyrn or Vortigern's Rock. He found it reassuring to be near Merlin who was the most sensible magician he had come across and the only one who ever managed to show him dragons.

Pryderi's Pigs

Once, so long ago that it can hardly be remembered, Math, the son of Mathonwy, was ruler of north Wales and Pryderi, the son of Pwyll, was ruler of south Wales. The stories of their lives are fractured like sunlight on water, full of half-lost whispers like the rustle of wind through dry grass.

One day Gwydion, Math's magician, came to him.

'Lord,' he said, 'I have heard that Pryderi, the son of Pwyll, has obtained a herd of wonderful creatures. They are smaller than oxen and their meat is much more tasty.'

Math was interested. He liked to hear tales of what his rival ruler was up to. He leant forward in his chair, eager to hear more.

'What are these new creatures called?' he asked.

'Pigs, my lord,' said Gwydion.

'Pigs?'

It was not a very exciting name, Math thought. He had expected better. Griffins, perhaps – part lion, part eagle. Gwydion sensed Math's disappointment.

'Sometimes they are called swine, my lord.'

'Swine?'

That was not a very exciting name either, Math thought. He had expected better. Basilisks, perhaps – part snake, part cockerel. Gwydion sensed Math's disappointment.

'Sometimes they are called hogs, my lord.'

'Hogs?'

That was not a very exciting name either, Math thought. He had expected better. Centaurs, perhaps – part man, part horse. Math was nervous of stories about griffins and basilisks and centaurs but at least they sounded exotic. A herd of animals called pigs or swine or hogs did not seem to match their glory. Still, Math was never happy for Pryderi to have something that he himself was lacking. It was obvious that the ruler who possessed these pigs could only increase his own power and importance.

The next day, at Math's command, Gwydion travelled south into the lands of Ceredigion which were ruled by Pryderi. He took eleven men with him and they were all dressed as poets and minstrels, rather than soldiers, so that they would be allowed to pass in peace. After a long journey, they came to Pryderi's palace which was set beside a broad river at a place called Rhuddlan Teifi.

Gwydion and his companions were welcomed into the palace and a feast was held that night in their honour. The tables groaned with the weight of food, rushlights flared and sputtered, their golden flame sending shadows dancing along the wall. Jug after jug of wine was carried in and dogs scrabbled for bones that were tossed on the floor. Gwydion's men sang, played their instruments, recited their poems and the evening passed merrily. Gwydion sat beside Pryderi. He entranced the company with such amusing and lively stories that Pryderi and the whole court were charmed by him. At the end of the evening, Gwydion turned to Pryderi and asked whether he might make a request.

'Certainly,' said Pryderi, smiling broadly and slapping him on the back. 'Anything that is mine to give, is yours for the asking.'

'Give me your herd of pigs,' said Gwydion boldly, 'so that I can take them with me into my own land and win favour with my lord.'

49

Pryderi pursed his lips and frowned.

'The pigs were given to me by Arawn, the king of Annwn,' he said. 'Because they come from the otherworld of Annwn, they are particularly rare and precious. Arawn made me promise that they would never be sold nor given away.'

Pryderi was relieved to be able to make this speech. He had grown fond of Gwydion during their jolly evening together but he did not want to lose his pigs. It was quite true that he had given his promise to Arawn and the king of the otherworld was not someone to be disobeyed.

'Make another request,' he offered generously. 'Anything else that is mine to give, is yours for the asking.'

Gwydion shook his head.

'It is the pigs I want,' he said, 'and the pigs I shall have. You say you are forbidden to give them to me, and you say you are forbidden to sell them to me. The king of Annwn has forbidden these things, but he has not forbidden you to exchange them for something else.'

Gwydion stood up and strode across the hall towards the door.

'I will meet you in the morning at the river's ford,' he said over his shoulder. 'Bring your pigs, for I will bring you something worthy of their exchange.'

Gwydion and his men rode back to their camp on the far side of the river.

'What have we got that we can offer in exchange for Pryderi's pigs?' Gwydion's men asked. 'It's useless. We've got nothing that could possibly tempt him.'

The men settled down despondently to sleep.

Gwydion did not sleep. All night he walked among the trees that bordered the river. His chanting echoed the song of the breeze in their branches. He slivered silver bark from a birch. He netted the midnight gleam of the moon. He caught each muscular movement of water. Copper earth, garnet berries, gilded grass. He scraped and gathered and bound them together. He re-shaped them with his hands, gave them life with the spell of his breath.

When Gwydion's companions woke in the morning, they were amazed at the sight that met their eyes.

Gwydion had conjured twelve chargers. They stood on the river's edge, silver as dawn. Their hooves struck shining spray from the shallows as they bent to drink. Their manes were long and fine as flax. Each horse had stirrups and a bridle of gold instead of iron. Their saddles were studded with precious stones. Beside the horses ran twelve greyhounds. They wore jewelled collars. Their coats were the velvet of night and each had a blaze like starshine on its breast.

Gwydion and Pryderi met at the ford in the river. Pryderi and his courtiers stood on the side closest to their palace. The herd of pigs snuffled and snorted around their feet. Gwydion and his companions stood on the side closest to their camp. The chargers and greyhounds stood with them, quivering with beauty and magic.

Pryderi could not take his eyes off them. He had never seen creatures so fabulous. Any mythical beast he had ever heard of, any griffin or basilisk or centaur, any wyvern or unicorn or phoenix, was as nothing compared

to these chargers and greyhounds offered to him. They outshone every living thing. They certainly outshone the herd of pigs he had received from the king of Annwn.

He agreed to the exchange.

The pigs crossed the river to Gwydion and the chargers and greyhounds crossed the river to Pryderi.

Gwydion raised his hand in farewell to Pryderi and a smile played around his lips. He ordered his men to mount their horses. They set off towards the north at once, driving the pigs before them.

'Faster, faster,' said Gwydion. 'We want to be as far away as possible by nightfall.'

Pryderi hardly noticed their going. He gloated over his greyhounds and chargers. All day he stayed with them in the river meadow. He stroked their flanks, murmured his love to them, wondered at the workmanship of each saddle and collar.

At twilight, Pryderi noticed a fading of the sheen on the creatures' coats, a dimming of the brilliance of their gems, a tarnishing of their silver and gold. At first he thought it was his own eyes playing tricks in the half-light, but the creatures continued to fade. It grew darker. The chargers were shadowy, the greyhounds like ghosts. Their pale shapes moved around him, insubstantial and soft as a sigh.

Pryderi called for flares to be brought from the palace. By the time they arrived, the animals had completely disappeared. Pryderi grabbed a flare and held it high. There was nothing to be seen – just a scattering of earth and berries and bark, a twist of hay, a distant glint of water and moon.

Hunting the Hare

An old woman and her grandson lived in a cottage on the lower slopes of Snowdon. The cottage was small but had stout, stone walls and a sound, slate roof. The old woman and her grandson were always cosy, even when winter storms howled around them. The old woman was poor but plump as a plum, her cheeks rosy as apples, her eyes bright as berries. She wore a blue skirt and a yellow blouse. People from the village would look up to see her moving about the mountainside. Her clothes were vivid as speedwell and celandine in the grass, cheery as sunshine in a summer sky.

Each day, Twm, the grandson, set off to work in the gardens of a grand house nearby. Each day, his grandmother tended the herbs and aromatic plants that she grew in her own garden. In every season, she also went out to gather leaves and roots, fruits and fungi, nuts and seeds that grew in the countryside around her cottage. Her kitchen steamed and bubbled with warmth and strange scents. She made cordials and jellies, perfumed potions, syrups and salves. Her neighbours would climb up the hill to call on her if they were ill. A sip of one of her ruby remedies, a spoonful of spicy mixture or the balm of her soothing creams, would soon cure their problems.

Twm and his grandmother loved animals. Twm loved to watch the wide-winged wheel of a buzzard, the slick somersault of trout in the stream. His grandmother loved the proud passing of the vixen, red against the hedge, the swoop of the flower-faced owl whose cry held the chill of snowfall. Most of all, Twm and his grandmother loved hares. The fields below the cottage were full of hares, full of the sudden bursts of their long-legged speed. Every evening, hares ran, faster than the race of cloud-shadow, across the hill. Twm would find the warm impression of a form where a hare had lain in the long grass. His grandmother would find a nest of leverets. The young hares gazed at her, eyes milky as moon, as she traced the tips of their silken ears with her finger.

The squire at the grand house where Twm worked loved hunting hares. One day he invited friends to join him in the sport. Twm was asked to lead the gentlemen to the fields near his cottage where hares were so often seen.

Twm brought the gentlemen down the valley road and then along the track that wound towards his home. As the hunting party climbed the hill, a hare dashed out from behind the cottage and ran across the field in front of them. It was a strange-looking hare, rather plumper than usual, with a rosy, russet tinge to its fur. If the huntsmen had been close enough, they might have noticed that the hare's eyes held the brilliance of berries rather than the sheen of the moon.

The huntsmen unleashed their greyhounds and sounded a blast on their horn. They gave chase to the hare. The hare led them a merry dance, racing over meadows, darting round rocks and leaping over streams. The hare would disappear into long grass or behind boulders and then reappear once more, as if by magic, in a different place. Wherever it was, the hare was always just out of reach of the dogs. Each time the hare was sighted, the horn shrilled through the valley and the dogs bayed as they again gave chase.

The huntsmen were soon exhausted but the hare never seemed to tire. It dashed and danced, twisted and turned, speeding so fast that its feet barely brushed the ground. At last, as dusk fell, the hunting party found themselves back once more close to Twm's cottage and the hare vanished completely.

'No kill,' puffed the squire, 'but a good day's sport.'

He gave Twm a silver coin for his help in the chase.

Time after time, whenever the gentlemen decided to hunt hare, the same thing happened. No hare would be seen except the plump, russet-tinged hare. The hunt would begin and end near Twm's cottage and the hare would never be caught.

'No kill,' the squire would puff, 'but a good day's sport.'

Time after time, Twm smiled politely and thanked

the squire for his silver coin. After a while, the gentlemen became suspicious.

'That valley's packed with hares, like plums in a pudding,' said the first, 'until we arrive. Then there's only one, one that no one can catch.'

'That valley's packed with hares, like apples in a pie,' said another, 'until we arrive. Then there's only one, one that no one can catch.'

'That valley's packed with hares, like berries on a bramble,' said a third, 'until we arrive. Then there's only one, one that no one can catch.'

The gentlemen began to look askance at Twm. They looked at his grandmother too and noted her plummy plumpness, her russet cheeks, her berry-bright eyes. They remembered the hare. They whispered amongst themselves. Their whispers were full of

'Witch, witch, witch.'

The gentlemen scowled at Twm's grandmother. They noted her cauldrons and potions, they noted her healing

the sick. They whispered amongst themselves and their whispers grew louder,

'Witch! Witch! Witch!'

The gentlemen knew witches were close to animals. The gentlemen knew witches could change shape. The gentlemen knew that only a pure, black greyhound could catch such a witch, such a shape.

The squire and his friends searched far and wide until they managed to find a suitable dog. The greyhound was slim and very fast, his pointed teeth glinted and his coat shone darkly as if it had been oiled.

Twm was asked to lead the huntsmen in their search for hare as usual. They had the black dog with them this time. As the huntsmen neared the cottage, the plump, russet, berry-eyed hare appeared. The hunters sounded their horn. The black dog strained at his leash until he was released and blazed up the hill after the hare. The hare tore away from him. Both were very fast, both seemed tireless as they sped and dodged and zig-zagged. The dog was always just one snap away from the hare's heels. Twm and the huntsmen watched.

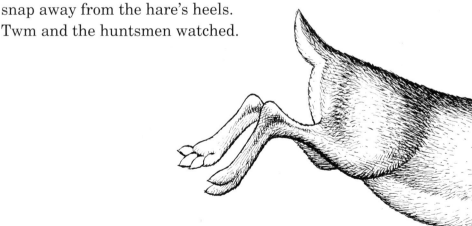

'Hei, gi du!' urged the hunters, encouraging the black dog.

'Hei, Mam-gu!' yelled Twm, forgetting himself and cheering on his grandmother in her hare shape.

It was impossible to tell which creature would win.

'Hei, gi du!'

The huntsmen were making themselves hoarse with shouting.

'Hei, Mam-gu!'

Twm shrieked with excitement.

The chase went on and on, to and fro, up and down, round and round the mountain meadows. The hare and dog were getting dizzy. Once the hare stumbled.

'Hei, Mam-gu!' called Twm as it recovered and raced on.

Once the dog tumbled down a bank.

'Hei, gi du!' called the hunters as it recovered and raced on.

On and on, to and fro, up and down, round and round. Round and round, down and up, fro and to, on and on. On and on. As dusk fell, the hare headed back towards the cottage. The black dog was right behind it. The two creatures spun and spiralled round and round the cottage. Twm knew that his grandmother was finding that she had no time to slow down and slip inside because the black dog was so close.

Round and round they went, then the hare shot into the front

60

garden and took a leap through the half-open window. The black dog soared into the air behind her. The huntsmen heard the dog's teeth clash shut as he missed the flying hare by centimetres and crashed against the window frame.

The dog lay, panting and exhausted beside the cottage wall. The squire and the huntsmen rushed through the garden and smashed open the front door. Twm followed. The men crammed into the cottage kitchen and then drew back in fright.

A hare sat in an armchair beside the fire. As they watched, it grew and grew until it filled the chair. Its fur smoothed slowly into rosy skin. Its long ears, sharp head, blurred to become the face of an old woman. Its strong legs were lost beneath a blue skirt, its paws became hands that smoothed a buttercup blouse.

Twm's grandmother smiled her sweet smile at the squire and his friends but some energy sparked and flashed about her. The room vibrated with magic. The huntsmen covered their ears against the high-strung song of it. The old woman's coloured mixtures and potions spun like a kaleidoscope of light. Motes of dust were spangled with stars and flames flared emerald in the fireplace. The huntsmen tried to cover their eyes as well as their ears and backed out of the cottage. They stumbled away down the valley, taking the black dog with them.

Later, Twm and his grandmother sat on a bench in the garden eating bread and cheese for supper.

'Hei, Mam-gu!' sighed Twm, shaking his head with a grin.

His grandmother didn't answer. She sat and watched the hares below as they moved swiftly, like wind, like cloud, like rain-squall across the fields.